I0726207

Adventures of the Saci Kids

A New Home

Pamella A. Russell

WORKBOOK PRESS LLC
187 E Warm Springs Rd,
Suite B285, Las Vegas, NV 89119, USA
Website: https://workbookpress.com
Hotline: 1-888-818-4856
E-mail: admin@workbookpress.com

Ordering Information:
Quantity sales. Special discounts are available on quantity purchases by corporations, associations, and others.
For details, contact the publisher and the author at the address above.

Library of Congress Control Number: 2016904507

ISBN-13:   978-1-958176-26-9 (Paperback Version)
                978-1-958176-27-6 (Digital Version)

REV. DATE: 01/05/2022

ADVENTURES OF THE SACI KIDS

A NEW HOME

PAMELLA A. RUSSELL

TABLE OF CONTENTS

Dedicated to all my families:

My parents, Olga Rose Uhl and William Franklyn Ryan

My adoptive Brazilian family, The Cacceses

My daughter, Carmen Rae Stanton Belardo and grandkids
(Alexander, Kevin, Ryan, Francis, Emmalee, Elliott, Gideon,
& Alex B)

My dearest friend, Maria de Lourdes Carvalho Prado
Ferraz

My Prado *foster* home – (Mãe Rita, João e Leonilda,
Maricota, Mifia e Ernesto, Lourdes, Roberto, Lena, Edson,
& Sergio)

My Russell family in its entirety

My wonderful husband, my very special Sací,
Robert J. Russell

*A lenda é como a miragem que o visionário assiste
existe mas não se nota ou se nota e não existe portanto
é numa miragem que a lenda se consiste.*

– Gonçalo Ferreira da Silva, Author

The legend is like a mirage that the visionary sees it
exists but is not noticed or noticed and does not exist
thus it is in a mirage that the legend is contained.

– Pamella A. Russell

PREFACE

As a teenager and young adult, I lived in Brazil for over six years where I fell in love with the Brazilian people, culture, language, music, and especially their rich folklore. Many years later I received my Masters in Library Service from Rutgers University's School of Communication, Information, and Library Studies. I am also a graduate from the Institute of Children's Literature. I especially love children's multicultural literature – books that tell an excellent story, are entertaining, and that teach something about people, life, love, pain, and the world around us. My favorite stories are of young people that in some manner, exhibit great courage, whether through adventures, disasters, by overcoming hardships, loving the unlovable, struggling through problems and failures, but always reaching beyond the limits of their abilities and endurance until they achieve their ultimate goals.

Fairy tales, folktales, and legends appeal to most of us no matter what age we are. So it is with the legend of Saci, a mythological character that developed among the African slaves brought to Brazil by the Portuguese to work in their large sugar plantations. In *Adventures of the Saci Kids: A New Home*, a chapter book aimed at ages nine to twelve, I have tried to share bits of the legend with my readers, while at the same time making him slightly unique to this story. He is my favorite Brazilian folk character, a trickster, whose mischievous pranks were made famous by the renowned Brazilian author Monteiro Lobato (1882-1948).

Folktales speak to all aspects of life and station – racial barriers, socio-economic issues, predicaments and choices, the challenges of families, to name a few. They accomplish this often through use of comedy, pranks, frightening events, mysteries, life lessons, plain entertainment, and through stories that are passed down for generations. For the most part, our protagonists overcome all obstacles, grow, and find joy, resolution, friendship, and love.

Let me know what you liked and what you didn't like about my story. Tell me what you think of the characters, especially little Sací. You may reach me at <u>pamrussell2@comcast.net</u> . I would love to hear from you.

ACKNOWLEDGMENTS

I would like to thank my husband, Robert J. Russell, for his proof reading, encouragement, and helpful suggestions.

CHAPTER 1

BURIED TREASURES

The beach was deserted. Yesterday's storm had left it littered with debris. Holly walked backward with her sandals dangling from her hand. She watched the narrow pattern her bare feet printed in the wet, slate-colored sand. One minute the footprints were there, the next minute they disappeared as the thick, ivory-yellow foam of the ocean rolled them out to sea. This reminded her of when her mother used to bake pies. Holly would make designs in the dough then her mother would smooth them out with the rolling pin. Those were happy memories—before her father was arrested for hurting her mother—before her life fell apart.

Holly walked back to the dry sand. It felt warm and gritty between her toes. She sat facing the gentle breeze of the late afternoon. She liked the way it lifted her short curls away from her face. She leaned into the wind as the tide pulled the salty water up onto the sand and then dragged the sand back into itself. She licked the salt from her lips and smiled at the seagulls standing watch along a stone jetty that rose from the sea.

Holly reached into the back pocket of her shorts for her diary. She unlocked it with one of the tiny gold keys she wore on a chain around her neck, along with a delicate crucifix, a confirmation gift from her mother. The chain also held a tiny gold medal of Our Lady *Aparecida* (who appeared) given to her by her favorite priest who had served as a missionary to Brazil. He explained its legend to her.

It had to do with some men fishing in a river, trying to catch fish for a feast being held in someone's honor. They prayed to Our Lady of the Immaculate Conception to give them a good catch. They were having no success and were ready to give up when, to their amazement, they fished up a broken statue of Our Lady of the Immaculate Conception. However, when they cleaned her she was black, so they decided to name her Our Lady Who Appeared. They wrapped the image carefully and thereafter began catching fish until their nets were full. It was considered a miracle. Holly wasn't sure if she believed in miracles.

She began leafing through her diary. She kept others just like it in her room, locked in a cedar chest that had belonged to her mother. For the past three years, her diaries had been her closest friends. Writing gave her strength. Through the written word, she could leave her fears and shyness behind, stand up for herself in any situation, and find the boldness and power to shape her life as she saw fit—the past, the present, and the future. Writing gave her command over her destiny and that of those she loved. Unlike life, writing gave her control over her story. Soon school would begin. Holly would be entering seventh grade this year. "Another new school. Another new family," she wrote in her diary. She remembered the day when Social Services had taken her to meet her first foster family. It was the same day her father had struck her mother repeatedly on the head and shoulders with the rolling pin while her mother had been baking. Holly had hidden behind the living room sofa and quietly dialed 911. The police had arrested her father and drove him off to jail in handcuffs. The ambulance had carried her mother's injured body to the hospital. Whenever she thought of this, her chest ached and her eyes burned from trying to hold back tears. When the police had asked Holly if she knew why her father had assaulted her mother, she had said it was because her mother wasn't making the pie he liked. That was three years ago. This was her third foster home since then. She hoped it was to be her last. She wondered when her father would be paroled and if her mother would someday recover her loss of memory. She questioned if they would ever be a family again and struggled with the conflicting answers.

Holly inhaled deeply of the sea air. There was a healing quality to the rhythmic sound of the waves smacking against the sand, to the seagulls raucously calling out to each other, to the loneliness, the stillness, and the peace. She pushed herself up from the now shadowy sand with alarm as she realized that the sun had dipped low in the sky over the bay side of the island. Mom and Pop Spears, her new foster parents, would be worried, wondering where she was and what was taking her so long.

Holly tucked her diary away and began running through the sand toward the road. Something dark, peaking out of the sand dunes, caught her eye. It was almost hidden by the thick beach grass. The dunes were off limits, but her curiosity outweighed the rules. Taking careful steps through the grass, she walked up to it. It was the top of a small wooden barrel, poking out of the sand dune. The storm must have washed it ashore.

Holly pulled at the barrel, but the sand sucked it back and held it captive—a prisoner to its surroundings, like herself. She scooped the sand away from around it and pulled again. A large cork jutted out from the side. She grabbed it and pulled with all her strength. She pulled so hard that when the barrel broke free of the sand, they both went rolling down the dune. Holly sat up at the bottom of the dune, clutching the cork in her hand with the barrel resting at her feet. The cork was bearing a sign of the cross. What could that possibly mean? Anxious to return home, Holly jammed the cork into her pocket and placed the barrel upright.

It stood about eighteen inches high and was surrounded by bands of metal that looked like brass. It looked old but appeared to be in good condition. Peering into the opening in the barrel, it seemed to be empty except she thought she could hear something rolling around inside making peculiar noises. Strange! Whatever was in there sure didn't smell so good!

Suddenly, an eerie, whistling emerged from the barrel, like someone mourning for the dead and exhaling the sound through shadowy graveyards. A shiver passed through Holly's body. What extraordinary events had brought this wooden barrel to rest on these quiet sandy shores? Holly heaved the barrel up onto her shoulder. She would need more time to examine it and to explore the mysterious sounds connected to it.

Chapter 2

Blended Families

Holly crossed the dirt road over to the bay side of the island. She quickly made her way through the watery marshes toward the large barn on Mom and Pop Spears' property. After placing the barrel inside the barn near the tractor and the bikes, she then hurried toward the house. It was an old three-story, five-bedroom farmhouse, the color of butterscotch pudding. Over the years, it had housed many foster children because Mom and Pop Spears had no children of their own. Some children were returned to their parents, some were eventually adopted, some just grew old enough to become independent. One thing certain, while they were living under Mom and Pop Spear's roof, they were loved and treated with good old Eastern Shore hospitality.

"Sorry I'm late for dinner," Holly apologized as she hurried through the back door.

"Just you come on in, sweetie, and rest your coat awhile!" Mom Spears shouted, waving her potholder toward the ceiling. "I've cooked ya'll the bestest dinner on the Eastern Shore—my award-winnin' chicken and dumplins' with peas. It won me $500.00 over to that there chicken festival last year. There'll be no famine in this house. The good book says, *He provides us with plenty of food and fills our hearts with joy.* Praise the Lord!"

Mom Spears placed the last of the steaming casseroles on the table. With a sweep of her large hand, she pushed the bangs away from her damp forehead and adjusted her bifocals. Her long colorful skirts billowed out around her broad hips while her brown oxfords carried her thick ankles across the kitchen.

"That's Eastern Shore talk for *you're welcome at our table, we're gonna eat yummy food, and we're gonna thank God for it!*" Ethan explained as Holly joined the three kids already seated around the long supper table. She knew a little bit about Ethan from Mom Spears. He was thirteen and the oldest foster child living with Mom and Pop Spears. His father was serving a life sentence in prison for a crime he said he didn't commit, his mother had died in a homeless shelter, and he had been separated from his two brothers and a sister who were all living in different foster homes. That had to be rough. He had a lot to prove.

Holly noticed the book beside his plate. "What are you reading?"

"Roots," he answered. "I want to know more about my ancestors because some day I'm gonna be an African-American history teacher."

"Cool," Holly said, sensing from his intensity that he had a passion for his heritage. "Where's Pop Spears?" she asked, looking down the supper table.

"Yonder, at the plant, tendin' to his duties." Mom Spears heaved her thick, fawn-colored braid off her shoulder. It cascaded down her back, past her waist. "Ever since Pop become manager of that there chicken plant acrost town, he don't spend near enough time to home. Says it's just takin' him a while to get the smart of it. But I can't complain. Bless his heart," she chuckled, "that's where all this finger-lickin' chicken come from. Best thing I ever put in my mouth." Her long silver earrings dangled and jingled from her pierced ears like wind chimes in yesterday's Nor'easter. "Grab hands! Ethan, you're the oldest. Ask the blessin'!"

Ethan's round brown face turned instantly red. His black eyes blinked nervously down the table at Mom Spears and the others. Nevertheless, Holly watched him bow his head. It was covered with a great crop of tightly curled black dread locks. The hand that stretched out to hold hers was thick, powerful, and callused. He ended the brief blessing with "Bless the homeless, the unjustly imprisoned, and all black brothers and sisters! Amen!"

"Amen!" Holly, Ashley, and Mom Spears joined in unison.

"There he goes with the black brothers and sisters, again," twelve-year-old Drew said, as he rolled his eyes toward the ceiling. His straight light-colored hair, fair skin, and gray eyes gave him an affluent look, as if he belonged on a golf course, or a sailboat. He was tall and lean. The cap he wore bore the Nike insignia. It had been autographed by Tiger Woods.

Mom Spears licked her fingers. "Now just never you mind, Drew Daniels! *The Lord is a refuge for the oppressed, a stronghold in times of trouble.* Ain't nobody ought to know that better than you. Ain't I right, darlin'? Mom Spears grabbed Drew's hand, giving it an affectionate squeeze. He quickly pulled his hand away and wiped it off. Despite Drew's grown-up appearance, he was *only* twelve. Holly knew he had been orphaned when his parents were killed in a plane crash. He was quiet and appeared detached from everyone, but she wondered if his indifference was his self-protection.

"Holly honey, stop your dreamin' and take some more chicken. You'll never be a writer if you don't feed your brain." Mom Spears pushed the platter of fried chicken in front of Holly.

"Where's the dog?" Eight-year-old Ashley asked. "Thought I heard something," she said, balancing on tiptoes. Her yellow-speckled, brown eyes held a startled expression. Her creamy complexion emphasized the freckles that spread across the bridge of her small round nose, and spilled over onto her cheekbones. She was wearing a faded turquoise cotton sweat suit that her scrawny body had outgrown long ago. Black-and-white-spotted Dalmatians jumped around the words "Puppy Love," written in pink letters on the front of her shirt. She wore tight turquoise socks that stretched up to meet the frayed edges of her shrunken pants. She tossed a Barbie doll on the table and darted toward the back door in her high-top, light-up sneakers. Heel, toe, heel, toe, she bounced in rhythmic steps, lighting up the back of one heel in florescent pink—the other heel remained dark, missing the beat.

Passing the dish of peas to Drew, Mom Spears shouted after Ashley. "Child, you just get right back here and eat your dinner. That critter can fend for hisself," Mom Spears grabbed for Drew's hat but missed. "Drew, take that confounded hat of yours off whilst you're at my dinner table, right quick!"

"He can't do that!" Ethan grinned. "His brains are in there!"

Drew threw a drop-dead look at Ethan across the table as he removed his hat and placed it carefully under his chair.

"I'm not hungry." Ashley sprinted back to the table where she threw her arms around Mom Spears' lap. She quickly planted a wet kiss on her knee, mumbled "I love you," then dashed in the direction of the backyard in search of Boswell, the family dog.

"Oh, my blessed! If that child's arms get any skinnier. . ." Mom Spears shook her head. "That ADHD thing don't let her sit down to table long enough to take nourishment."

Holly's fork paused on its way to her mouth. "I went to school with a girl who had ADHD. Every afternoon she was called down to the nurse's office to take her medication. She had a hard time sitting still, and the teacher had to keep telling her to pay attention. She said the girl had *poor listening skills.*"

Mom Spears sat back nodding her head up and down like a bobble-head doll. "Doc says it means attention deficit hyperactivity disorder. I say it means she don't pay no heed and can't never stop movin'."

Ashley burst through the door, dragging a reluctant, bellowing beagle on a ragged leash. "Boswell's dog food is all over the backyard. Poor thing. He couldn't find his dinner." She dropped the leash and abandoned the nervous dog, which quickly ran and hid under the table. Grabbing a pencil and tablet, she began to draw at the kitchen table. She concentrated on her drawing while at the same time scratching her face and pushing strands of sparse chestnut-brown hair out of her mouth. Her needle straight bangs poked over her scant eyebrows. At the crown of her head was a slightly bald area where wisps of short, broken hair pointed upward.

"Ash, what happened to the hair at the top of your head?" Holly asked, as she ran her fingers through the stubby sprouts.

"She used to pull it," Ashley answered, chewing on her bottom lip.

"She who?"

"Grandma. And it really hurt." Ashley imitated the action by pulling up at the oily strands. "But she never stopped. I kept telling her to stop but she always pulled it any way." Leaning over her picture, she pushed her hair behind her round slightly protruding ears. They bore piercings, but no earrings.

Ashley suddenly dropped her pencil and scrambled off the chair. She leaped around the table like a roadrunner—a florescent flash with long black feet, aiming herself in Mom Spears' direction. Ashley demanded her immediate attention by leaning up against her and whispering loudly into her ear. "Mom, can I have a pudding?"

Placing her arm around Ashley and pulling her onto her lap, Mom Spears continued speaking to Holly. "That's how I come to get her. School reported the abuse to Social Services, and they paid a little visit to Grandma. Found the child tied in a chair. Grandma said that was the ownliest way she could get her housework done because the kid wouldn't stop gettin' into things. Imagine! Why do you think the good book says, *Suffer the little children...* God knew they was goin' to get into things and grown-ups was gonna suffer!"

Ashley, cupping her hand around Mom Spears' ear, at full

volume whispered more insistently. "Mom, can I have a pudding?" Badly chipped bright red nail polish covered her tiny fingernails.

"You already ate your puddin'." Gently setting Ashley back down on her *light-ups*, Mom Spears pushed back on her chair, most likely giving her body considerable room for digestion.

"Did not," Ashley mumbled as she scrambled under the table in the direction of Boswell. He dashed out from underneath, his nails slipping and sliding on the linoleum floor, and sat straight up on his hind legs and howled.

"Dog's acting strange," said Ethan. "Haven't seen Pitsa, either. She must be stalking mice." He shoveled dumplings into his mouth, three at a time.

"Slow down, brother! Ain't nobody goin' to take those dumplins' from you long as I'm around." Mom Spears let out a hearty laugh as she began to clear the table. "Let's get the evenin' chores done. Holly, you're the newest. Do the washin' up."

"I had to wash until you came along," Drew said grinning. "New guy always has to wash. Besides, it was hurting my image, to say nothing of my hands." He retrieved his cap from under his chair, positioned it on his head, boldly stood up, and took his golfer's stance as if to swing a club. Then looking slightly embarrassed, he headed for the kitchen sink. Holly watched him walk over to the towel rack. Truth was, it was a bit hard to picture such a drop-dead gorgeous kid with a dishcloth in his hand.

Mom Spears aimed herself at the living room door while delegating the rest of the chores. "Ash, angel, come out from under that table and finish clearin'. Ethan, brother, you sweep. I'm gonna go sit myself a spell and knit. *If a man's hands are idle, the house leaks.*" Turning her head in the direction of the fireplace, she stopped short.

"Jist listen at all that noise! Sounds like wind whistlin' yonder through the gates of the cemetery." Mom Spears turned a ghostlike face back to the kids. Slowly, she rotated her body in the doorway and headed back into the kitchen toward the back stairs leading up to the bedrooms. "Sounds like spirits. Not a hardly do I want to hear from any of my people that passed this life! I'm wore out enough listenin' to the ones still livin'.'"

Holly glanced at the faces of the other three kids. They were watching Mom Spears climb the steps to her room. Holly wondered if the whistling sound in the house was the same as the whistling coming from the barrel. The other kids didn't know yet about the strange wooden barrel sitting out in the barn. They hadn't heard the mysterious whistling sound coming from it, a sound that made her soul ache. Holly's hands felt icy. Should this be her secret? What would the kids do if she told them? Tomorrow, she would have to investigate further.

CHAPTER 3

DEVILMENT

"Devilment, that's what this is—pure devilment."

"What's up, Mom Spears?" Holly stepped into the kitchen, rubbing the sleep from her puffy eyes. She stopped suddenly, shocked by the scene around her. Flour was spread all over the kitchen floor. There were traces of a solitary footprint the size of a toe making tracks to the back door. "What the...?"

"Devilment," Mom Spears said with her hands on her hips. She stood looking all around at the mess when Drew slammed through the kitchen door. His usual self-control had crumbled. "Thumper and Juniper are sound asleep in the corral, end to end, with their tails braided together. They look worn out and lathered, as if someone's been riding them all night!" he shouted.

Ethan walked in behind Drew with an empty milking pail and slammed it down on the table. "Molly's not going to give us any milk today! I don't know what's spooked her. I kept pulling on her, but she just kept mooing and stomping, and looking around with these big old frightened cow eyes." Ethan made a crazed, wide-eyed look that started everyone laughing even with the strangeness of the situation.

"Well, we have to eat somethin'. This dough I left out to rise is flat as a pancake." Mom Spears gave the deflated mound of bread dough a hard thump. "Holly honey run out to the hen house and grab us a couple of eggs. Leastways I can scramble us up some eggs for breakfast."

When Holly walked into the chicken coop, the layers were in an uproar, cackling at each other. Searching around, she found no eggs anywhere. She ran back to the house. "There's no eggs!" Holly leaned on the door frame, trying to catch her breath. "The hens are so upset. They're running all around the coup trying to hide and bumping into everything. Their feathers are all ruffled and puffed out. They wouldn't even squat for me to pet them!"

"Fright! Stress! There's devilment goin' on here. I can feel it in my bones." Mom Spears cried.

"My clothes are thrown everywhere." Ashley wailed, running into the kitchen. "Someone's opened all my dresser drawers and pulled all my clothes out." She ran over to Ethan and punched him in the side. "Bully! Why'd you do that?"

"Cut it out, nose picker! I didn't touch your creepy old clothes. I wouldn't want to catch whatever you've got!"

Ethan reached out to yank the wispy hair on the top of her head.

"Leave her be, Ethan Owens!" Mom Spears hollered

"How come nothing like this ever happened before you came here?" Drew stood tall and rigid, as he looked accusingly at Holly.

"Calamity Jane, that's what she is," Ethan put in. "A red-headed, green-eyed she-devil forcing mayhem on all of us."

"Hush! I don't want to hear that kinda' talk. We're a family. Families stick together, no matter what. If any one of us is havin' a problem, we'll just love it out. We don't tough it out—we love it out." Mom Spears mopped the sweat off her face with her apron, leaving it streaked with flour.

Holly's face heated up. She ran for the door before she burst into tears. She saw Ashley's curious look as she ran by but didn't care. No one was going see her cry. Holly was angry, but most of all she was afraid. Once, she had fallen off the top of a sliding board in the school playground. She could still remember the feeling of helplessness when her arms had reached out to grab hold of something to stop the fall. Nothing had been there but air. Lying on her back under the sliding board, she had tried to breathe. All the kids in the playground had surrounded her, staring down at her while she had pulled and sucked at the air, trying to draw it back into her lungs.

The same feeling of panic overcame her now as she ran toward the barn to get her bike. She wanted desperately to be alone where no one could gawk at her struggle to contain her fear. Her tears blinded her as she ran. She tripped on a tree root, sending her sprawling on the ground. She lay there until the tears quieted. The sun's warmth dried her face and the breeze carried her into a memory of an earlier time.

It was a night when she was only eight. Her father wasn't home. Her mother had to work late and didn't like leaving her home alone, but she worked just across the street. Her mother had instructed her to call if anything strange happened and they would send a guard. What could happen? The streets were safe. People didn't lock their doors. But then something did happen – footsteps on the back stairs leading up to their apartment. Holly's heart had pounded as the footsteps grew stronger. The footsteps had reached the top landing. Holly had hardly been able to breath. There had been a knock. Holly had tried to be silent with her ear pressed to the door. She had heard someone breathing on the other side, another knock. She had felt faint like she might throw up. She had heard movement, hesitation, uncertainty, as though the person sensed that she was on the other side of the door. She had heard soft rustling noises, then the footsteps were slowly receding down the stairs. Had the person really left, or were they just pretending, hiding, hoping that she would open the door and they would catch her? She had run to the phone and dialed her mother. Minutes later, Holly had heard footsteps running up the driveway, then up the back stairs, followed by banging on the door. She had been grateful for the solid uniformed body that stood guarding her doorway. She had explained the spooky way the footsteps had come up the stairs; the quiet, eerie feeling she had felt. As the guard had turned to leave, both pairs of eyes simultaneously had registered on something in the corner of the landing. It was a huge tissue-papered package...flowers...a bouquet...someone...a florist. That was who had come up the stairs. A friend had sent them flowers.

How could something so innocent have caused such fear? Fear of the unknown, of what you couldn't see but could only imagine. Maybe that was all there was to the barrel. She picked herself up and headed toward the barn. The enemy was fear and she would conquer it!

Chapter 4

The Dust Devil

Holly pulled open the barn door. She went to Thumper's stall to greet him and stopped dead in her tracks. Two glowing red spots, like the bright red eyes of a snake, were aimed up at her from the dark corner of the stall. Coming from that direction was the same strange whistling sound she had noticed at the beach. The whistle grew so strong that the ground trembled and the barn shook. Instinctively, she grabbed for the overhead light switch. Whatever was hidden in the dark, spun into a whirlwind of dust, leaves, and straw and dissolved into thin air leaving behind a faint odor of rotten eggs.

Holly jumped on her bike and took off, leaving a trail of dirt flying behind. She had to tell the others. But what was it? There was no reasonable answer. Was that the *devilment* that had been causing all the mess? The kids would laugh at her. No one would believe her. They would think she made it up. She felt sick to her stomach but worse than that, she felt stupid because she couldn't figure out what she saw. So, how would she be able to explain it?

After riding in circles around the barn for what seemed like an hour, Holly decided she had to talk to someone. She headed in the direction of the dock to see if Drew had gone down to work on Pop Spears' fishing boat. The dock stretched out for some distance across the tideland to a shallow section of the bay.

"Drew!" Holly called out to him, setting the kickstand of her bike. Drew had his shirt off in the early morning sun, scrubbing down the seats with boat soap. He straightened up, pushing his light hair off his forehead with his arm. Soapy water trickled from the sponge onto his shoulder. He wiped it away with his thumb. As Holly neared him, she recognized the wary look on his face. "What's up?" he asked, turning his back to her. He splashed water on the seats from a bucket and began rubbing them down with a dry towel.

"Drew, it isn't me. I'm not the *devilment*. You need to believe me. I know it sounds crazy, but there's this thing in the barn with glowing eyes that stinks and whistles and makes everything shake. When I turned on the barn light, it changed into this mini tornado of dirt and stuff and just disappeared."

Drew laughed. "Yea, and it's called Holly's folly, right? A little folktale to write about in your diary. I can see it now. Holly McCabe, future famous writer."

"Hey, if it isn't the Drewster and carrot cake!" Ethan hollered as he strode down the dock toward them. Drew flung his damp towel on the floor of the boat. "Speaking of future famous people, here comes Dr. Owens, future professor of African-American history."

"What's up?" Ethan asked, glancing from one to the other as he walked up to them. He positioned his husky frame firmly in front of them, with feet set apart and arms akimbo.

"Nothing," Holly mumbled, while Drew gave her a curious look.

"Well anyway, I came out to get you guys. Mom Spears is going crazy. She says the house is cursed. All the knitting she worked on last night came unraveled. Every time she puts down her thimble or sewing scissors, she finds them in a different place when she goes to use them. She put a pot of soup on to cook for dinner and keeps finding the lid off the top of the pot. And something got into the sack of corn kernals and ate most of them so we won't have any popcorn for our Friday night movie." Ethan stood there, shaking his dreadlocks in disbelief. "Oh, and you know those funny golf balls you're always making, Drewster?" Holly looked at Drew's blank face for confirmation. "You know, the ones you make by cutting strips of plastic grocery bags and balling them up and wrapping masking tape around them? The ones Ashley keeps picking up all over the yard?"

"I get it, Ethan, what's your point?" Drew asked, impatiently.

"Well, someone got into the bucket full of them and they're laying everywhere, like the invasion of the snowballs. Mom

Spears is back at the house quoting scripture all over the place."
He made hand gestures looking like a preacher bringing down
the wrath of the Almighty at a summer revival meeting.

"Holly confessed it's the devil made her do it," Drew jerked his
thumb toward Holly. "Go ahead, tell Ethan what you told me.
See what he says about your little folktale."

"I'm telling you the truth." Holly stood facing Ethan with her
hands on her hips. "When I went out to the barn there was
this thing—this little thing—in Thumper's stall, glowing. Well,
its eyes were glowing. Bright red. It stunk like rotten eggs. I
heard this loud whistle that shook the barn. When I turned on
the light to get a better look, this wind tunnel formed spinning
around with dust and leaves and straw from Thumper's stall.
Then it just swirled away and disappeared." Holly heaved a
loud sigh.

"Man, that's a great story! How long did it take you to think
that one up?" Ethan glanced first at Holly and then Drew.

"Look, if you don't believe me, come with me to the barn and
see for yourselves. Maybe it's back," Holly challenged them.

Drew pulled on his shirt, then slapped his cap on his head
as he jumped onto the dock. He sprinted ahead, taking the
lead with Ethan stomping after him. Holly followed behind
on her bike; afraid the thing would be there and afraid that it
wouldn't. With a sudden surge of confidence, she pushed her
chin into the air and quickened her pedaling. She was ready to
face down the *devilment.*

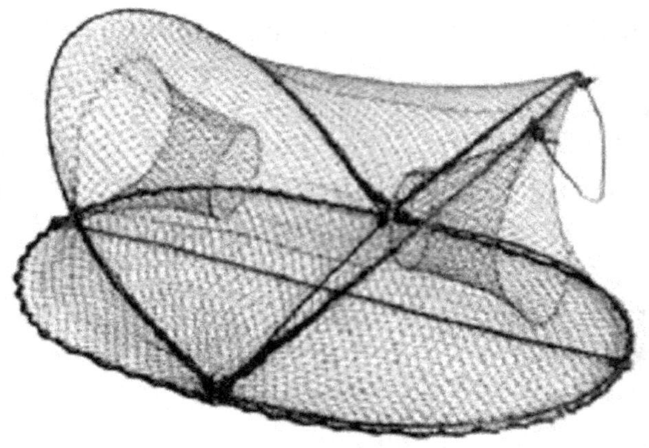

CHAPTER 5

SOMETHING CAGEY

Drew, Ethan, and Holly raced toward the barn. As they approached, Ashley ran up to them dragging Pitsa, the barn cat, in an egg crate.

"Where are you guys going?" she asked, dropping the crate.

"We're hunting down Holly's devil," Ethan bellowed, opening the barn door.

All four of them surged through the door at the same time, knocking each other aside. The smell lingered from earlier. They slid to a stop.

"Thumper and Juniper must have awful gas," Ashley said, holding her nose.

Holly moved nothing but her eyes, searching the dark corners low to the ground for two red dots. Nothing. Nothing looked unusual or out of place. No strange sounds came bursting forth to prove her right. Now what? "I'm telling you, there was this thing, glowing, stinking, spinning." Holly stood her ground.

"Yea, sure," Ethan, Drew, and Ashley said in unison as they turned away to leave the barn.

"Well, your fiction will sure be a best seller," Drew said, his voice dripping with sarcasm.

"Look! There it is!" Holly pointed down at two red dots outside of Thumper's stall.

Sure enough, they were there in one of the corners. Instantly, the smell of rotten eggs tainted the air. The whistling started. All together, they placed their hands over their ears to dull the sound. Suddenly, the barn began to shake. The whirlwind emerged, swirling dust, pieces of straw, and dead leaves.

This time, instead of grabbing the light switch, Holly grabbed a crab pot hanging on the wall of the barn. She tossed it over the whirlwind and it fell to the floor of the barn with a clatter. Something scrambled into the throat of the pot and up into the holding area.

"Take it out and see what it is!" Ethan poked Drew.

"You take it out!" Drew snapped, stepping slightly backwards.

"It stinks," Ashley whispered, furiously picking her nose.

Holly reached out and pulled Ashley's hand away from her face and slowly got down on her knees. The others followed her, surrounding the pot on four sides and kneeling low to the ground. All four faces pressed close to the wire cage. At first, all they could see was a bit of red wiggling around.

"What do you think it is?" Holly asked.

"It's an elf!" Ashley shouted, jumping up.

"Elves aren't black," Drew pointed out, looking closer.

"It's smaller than my shoe," Ethan exclaimed with a look of wonderment.

"The poor thing has only one leg, and he's not wearing anything but a red hat." Holly shivered. Gingerly, she reached into the crab pot to pull the creature out.

"It's naked!" Ashley gasped.

"Careful! It'll escape," Ethan said.

When Holly withdrew her hand, the only thing she was holding was his tiny red cap, shaped like a miniature gourd. Carefully, she reached again into the crab pot and lifted the elfin figure out. She seated him on the ground. He seemed dazed and scratched his head, looking all around.

The kids bombarded him with questions, over and over.

"Who are you?"

"What are you doing here?"

"When did you get here?"

"Where did you come from?"

"How did you get here?"

"Why were you playing tricks on us?" Ashley asked. *Sometimes she made the most sense*, Holly thought.

"*Cadê meu chapeu?*" the little guy asked, rubbing the top of his somewhat bald head.

"What did you say?" Ethan leaned closer.

The elf-like figure rose onto his one leg. *"Me dá meu chapeu!"* he shouted, hopping up and down.

"We don't understand you," Holly said.

"Vocês tiraram meu chapeu." The little guy sat down, pointed to his head where the hat had been and made angry noises and gestures.

"I think he wants his hat back," Holly said, reluctant to give up her keepsake. She memorized his characteristics so there would be a lot to write in her diary tonight. He had an impish face and was the color of a brown ant. He had ears like that of a bat, but not pointed. His shiny, lively eyes had black pigmentation in the center. The outer membranes were white like eggshells, but it appeared that when he got angry or felt threatened, they turned red like hot coals. He had a pot belly and only one leg with a tiny foot shaped like that of a human. His hair was sparse but curly. He had no clothes. In his right hand, he carried an empty pipe. He oozed a stench of rotten eggs.

"Maybe he uses that odor like a skunk uses its perfume—to ward off its enemies." Holly said. "What is your name?" She asked, softly.

He looked confused and shook his head. She pointed to herself and said "Holly." She pointed to the others— "Ethan, Drew, Ashley." Then she pointed at him.

"Saci. Me chamo Saci," he answered.

They looked at him questioningly. Holly imitated his pronunciation. "Sounds like Sa-SEE."

"Meu nome é Saci," he repeated, appearing agitated.

"It sounds a little like Spanish. I've studied it in school," Holly said. "I think he's trying to tell us that his name is Sací."

"Sací. I like the sound." Ashley whirled around in circles. "Sací-e-e. I love Sací."

"It figures," Ethan muttered.

"What will we do with him?" Drew asked.

"Well, we can't tell Mom and Pop Spears. Mom Spears will try to exorcise him," Ethan answered, pacing back and forth.

"Let's put him back in the barrel that I found on the beach. I think that's where he was living when I found him." Holly said.

"If he was the one causing the devilment, he'll just start getting into things, again," Ashley answered.

Holly shook her head. "Well, maybe not. When I found the barrel, there was a wooden cork sticking out of it. It came out when I pulled the barrel out of the sand. It was marked with a cross. I don't know if that means anything or if that's just coincidence. Anyway, I stuck it in my shorts pocket, and never thought to put it back."

"That's probably how he got out," Drew said. "Through the hole."

Holly jumped to her feet. "Wait, I'll go and get it."

She ran out of the barn to the house, went straight through the kitchen, and tiptoed up the steps, hoping Mom Spears wouldn't stop her. Upstairs, she rummaged through her laundry basket and found the shorts she had been wearing. Sure enough, the cork was right where she had put it. She rushed downstairs, through the kitchen, and escaped out the back door, unseen.

Holly shut the barn door behind her and held out the cork. "Drew, you put him in the barrel!"

"No, I don't want to touch it. Ethan, you do it!"

"No way, Drewster. I ain't into the prison principle. Ashley, you do it!"

Ashley kneeled down and gently scooped Sací into the palm of her hand. "It's okay, Sací. We won't hurt you. We just don't want you doing any more devilment." She patted his head. "Holly, are you going to put his hat back on? He might get cold."

Holly looked at the cap in her hand. "What if he tries to escape?" She examined the cap's unusual shape and noted its marvelous red color. Then she looked at Sací. The cap had to symbolize something important due to Sací's agitation at losing it. She knew how much Drew's cap meant to him— that and his Sunday red shirt. They were his most prized possessions. A smile barely began to twitch at the corners of Sací's mouth, but a mischievous twinkle in his eyes decided his fate.

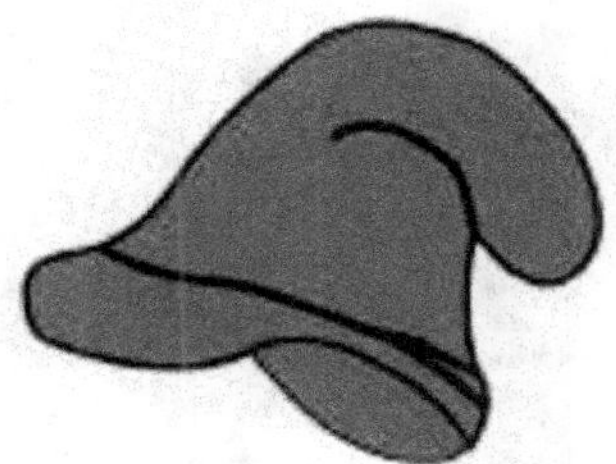

"No. I think I'll hold onto the cap for a while," Holly answered. "I'm not sure why, but I think this cap is important to Sací for a reason." She put the red cap in her pocket and helped Ashley squeeze Sací into the barrel through the opening.

She sealed the wooden barrel with the cork and placed it in a dark corner in the rear of the barn, where no one would see it.

"Tomorrow, let's all go to the library and see if we can discover who this little creature is." Holly suggested.

"Yea, we can Google *Sací* and see what comes up," Drew replied.

"Maybe there's something in an encyclopedia," Ethan added.

Ashley just jumped up and down, clapping her hands.

That night, Holly was so excited she could hardly sleep. Who was this creature? Where had he come from? What would they do with him? Hopefully tomorrow's trip to the library would reveal some answers.

CHAPTER 6

TO THE LIBRARY

The next day Holly, dressed in jeans and a sweatshirt, slipped out the back door of the house and greeted the quiet splendor of daybreak. At times, the bay smelled like an abandoned outhouse. Today the soft breezes moving across the water and over the tideland that made up several acres of the Spears' property hinted of the sweet smell of fresh watermelon. This was her favorite time of the day. She sat on the steps of the back porch and reminisced about the years when she attended Catholic middle school. She had loved to walk to school in the early morning and had often attended the Sisters' 7:00 a.m. mass. The open chapel doors and tall stained-glass windows would let in the smells and sounds of the early morning. These would blend with the waft of burning candles and the spicy scent of incense – a serene background for the whispered sounds of "Hail Mary, full of grace…" as deft fingers poking out of voluminous brown sleeves would move silently across black rosary beads.

The sounds of Thumper and Juniper neighing from the barn brought Holly abruptly back to the present. She wanted to check on Sací. She was worried that he might have suffocated in the barrel—foolish notion since he had probably come across the ocean confined in those close quarters. As she headed toward the barn, the sound of soft sneakers padding behind her caused her to turn around. Three grinning faces were trailing behind her in single file.

"I guess all of us had the same idea," she said, a little disappointed that the privacy of her mission had been invaded.

Once inside the barn, Holly retrieved the barrel and quickly removed the wooden cork. "Sací, are you there?" She called into the opening. Snores echoed from the barrel.

Holly replaced the cork. "Well, sure sounds like he's okay. I guess now would be as good a time as any to make that trip to the library."

Grabbing their bikes, Holly stopped to yell into the house. "We're off to the library. We won't be long."

The town library was small but automated. Ethan headed for the encyclopedias while Holly and Drew headed for the bank of computers. Ashley veered off to the children's section to see if she could find a picture of Sací.

As soon as Drew typed in *Sací* as a search term, a free online encyclopedia found a definition. "Holly, look what came up!" Holly peered over Drew's shoulder, checking out the screen.

Saci is a character in <u>Brazilian folklore</u>. He is a one-legged <u>black</u> or <u>mulatto youngster</u>, who smokes a <u>pipe</u> and *wears a magical red cap that enables him to disappear and reappear wherever he wishes (usually in the middle of a* dust devil*). Considered an annoying* prankster *in most parts of Brazil . . . he nevertheless grants wishes to anyone who manages to trap him or steal his magic cap... The legend says that a person can trap a Saci inside a dark bottle when he is in the form of a* dust devil*.*

"A legend? But Drew, that isn't just a legend that's inside that barrel. That's a real live Saci!" Holly whispered. "And what's a *dust devil*?"

"The article says it's caused by the spin-dance of an invisible Saci. It goes on to list all the pranks that Saci has been known to pull. A bunch of those we saw yesterday in our own house! It also says that Saci can be captured and lured into a dark bottle where he can be imprisoned by a cork with a cross on it. It goes on to say that his red cap is his source of power and if you steal it, he becomes your slave. But if you're good to him and return his cap, he'll become your friend and guardian forever. What are we dealing with here, Holly?" Drew asked.

"I don't know, but this is too weird. Saci wasn't in a bottle, he was in a dark barrel, but the cork did have a cross on it. I wondered what that was for. Let's go see if Ethan found anything in the encyclopedias." Holly pulled Drew over to the reading table. "Watcha got?"

Ethan was deep in thought as he feverishly wrote down everything he could find on the subject. "It looks like the Saci myth began in Europe, but the African plantation slaves in Brazil brought the character to life as a way of amusing the children as well as scaring them into obedience with 'Watch out for Saci!' A popular expression among Brazilian children whenever they misbehaved was 'Saci made me do it!'

The Sací myth was made popular in the 1930s by Monteiro Lobato, one of Brazil's most influential writers, especially of children's books."

"Where do you think our Sací came from? What country?" Drew asked.

"How are we going to help him find his way back home?" Holly asked.

"Is Sací lost?" Ashley asked. "I couldn't find any pictures of him. Should I draw one and post it on the lost-and-found board at the market?"

"I don't think that would be wise," Holly answered, giving Ashley a hug. "First, we need to see if we can get Sací to talk to us and tell us his story."

Holly wondered how they were going to understand him. Her Spanish wasn't that good, and she certainly didn't know any Portuguese. Maybe she could get a dictionary at the bookstore.

CHAPTER 7

PALM TREES AND SUGAR CANE

Come on out, Sací! We want to talk to you" Holly called. A long pipe emerged first then slowly the face that was attached to it poked through the hole of the barrel. Slowly, squeezing himself out with grunts and groans he managed to fit through the opening.

"Bom dia meus presados amigos," Sací said, smiling and bowing low to the ground. "Good morning, my dear friends, as you say in the English."

Holly's mouth dropped open. "How did you learn to speak English overnight? I thought I would have to find a Portuguese dictionary."

"I can do anything, most of the time. But especially if I

wear my red cap." Sací gazed up at Holly with eyes that were round like black cherries, and grinned. "My red cap it is gift from my father. When I wear it, I am Super Sací. I am invisible. I spin into whirlwind and travel anywhere, quickly. I am in many places at the same time. I am called Son of Wind. I am what you call shapeshifter. My favorite disguise is little songbird. But now, *you* have my red cap." He pointed the mouth of his pipe at the four kids. "So, I am yours. You are my masters. This is the way of the Sacís." He gave them a pitiful, deflated look. "I promise not to be bad-tempered. I will not play too many tricks on your people. I do not want that you give me fifty whippings a day or that you take away my beans and bananas."

"Where did you come from?" Ashley sat cross-legged on the ground. Holly thought she looked ready for a good story.

Sací leaped to the top of the barrel and sat resting on the hip where his other leg should have been and dangled his one and only leg over the side. He looked calm and relaxed. He didn't seem to mind that he was missing a limb.

The kids all settled themselves comfortably around Sací while he told them his story.

"I am from Brazil. Tupi-Guarani Indians call it *Land of Palm Trees*. Sací is Tupi Indian name. We were born by burning campfires of African slaves in Brazilian brushwood. Slaves tell stories to children about Sací. On cold nights in June when is Feast of St. John, we sing and dance and play many tricks on each other. We are band of tricksters. We pester masters of sugar plantations. My band of Sací live in brushwood. We hide at edge of water in cracks of stones where ferns guard entrance to our caves." Sací's body shivered. "But we no cross water. Sací have fear to cross water. By day, we sit on branches of old trees and smoke our pipes and drink sugar cane rum. By night, we come out of hiding from caves. We call with our whistle and begin nighttime tricks on plantation masters and innocent travelers."

"That's why the tails of Thumper and Juniper were braided together," Drew said.

"And why Molly wouldn't give us any milk," Ethan exclaimed.

"The hens wouldn't lay any eggs, either" Holly added.

"That's why Boswell was acting so weird and why his dog food was spread all over the yard," Ashley said. "You should be ashamed of yourself, Sací. Everyone blamed Holly for your tricks."

"Even Mother Spears was in a state because you ruined her reputation as the best cook on the Eastern Shore." Holly laughed. She felt such relief now that the kids knew she wasn't to blame for all the *devilment.*

"I know." Sací clapped his hands gleefully. He bolted down off the barrel and hopped up and down on his solitary leg. "Cee-e-e." He laughed in a thin, whistling manner, like the sound of wind sighing through the leaves of the trees.

"How did you lose your leg, Sací?" Ashley asked.

"I never lose leg! I only ever have one. All Sací have only one leg. But we jump along on that leg faster than you can run. Besides, is easier to sit on your shoulder and whisper in your ear." With that, he sprang up to Ashley's shoulder, put his tiny, black hand at the side of his mouth with his fingers pressed tightly together and jutting straight out to touch her face in front of her ear, and whispered something none of the others could hear. Ashley's eyebrows rose as she swallowed a gulp of air.

"Cee-e-e." Sací looked pleased with himself.

"What did he say, Ash?" Holly asked.

"It is secret. It is secret." Sací slid down her shoulder and bounced up and down on the ground. "Cannot tell secrets. Cee-e-e!"

"She'll tell," Ethan said. "Ashley's got a big mouth. She tells everything."

"Do not," Ashley looked down scraping her shoe against the barn floor.

"Do too." Drew pushed his Nike cap to the back of his head.

"Ashley will tell us when she's ready, won't you Ash?" Holly put a hand on Ashley's shoulder.

"He told me to get his red cap from you, Holly," Ashley blurted out. Sací threw his pipe on the ground and began walking in circles.

"Sací, you still haven't told us how you got here." Ethan said.

"My clan throw me out because I am different—I no smoke my pipe, I only carry it to look same as other Sací. But I do like to blow bubbles from it. I no drink the sugar cane rum either. I like the coconut milk, better. I am also too much likable." Sací grinned at the kids and his black cherry eyes twinkled. "I no make tricks on masters that hurt them. I only make tricks to confuse them."

"You sure confused us," Holly said.

Ethan leaned forward, "but you still haven't told us how you got here."

"I am saved by African slave boy. His name is Moco. He

work on large sugar plantation near where I hide. His parents work the sugar-mills. His grandparents were Bantus. One day, the Portuguese took them on ship from their home in Angola in South West Africa to Salvador, the capital of Bahia in Brazil to work the sugar cane plantations in New World colony. Millions of slaves go to Brazil from Africa." Saci said.

"I thought only America had slaves," Ethan exclaimed.

"No, Brazil had, too. One day, Moco is taken from plantation and put on ship with hundreds other slaves going to Florida. He hide me in his pocket and take me with him. The problem is I afraid of water." Saci sat down, his shoulders rounded, his head shaking from side to side. "I have so much fear and I am so seasick that I climb into empty rum barrel and hide there. Someone put cork into hole and seal me inside. Fumes from rum give me nice long sleep. I think barrel fall into water and now I am here. Poor Moco. Mayby he look for me everywhere. That is all I remember."

"I'm sorry, Saci," Holly said. "You must miss him."

Saci began to sing. "Sa...cee!" "Sa...cee!" Holly thought that the song had a sad, homesick, rhythmical sound—like that of a little bird singing in the depths of the dark Brazilian brushwood, remembering those cold nights in June by the blazing campfires of the Feast of St. John.

Suddenly, Holly raised her head, listening. She heard footsteps outside the barn. Ashley must have heard them, too, because she ran to the barn door.

"Hi! Mr. Drudge! What are you doing here?" Ashley asked in a high-pitched voice, blocking his entrance to the doorway.

With an athlete's speed, Drew scooped up Saci, shoved him into the barrel, and pushed the cork in place. Drew, Ethan, and Holly placed themselves in front of the barrel and stood guard over their prized possession as Henry Drudge, the town scavenger and antique dealer, bullied his way through Ashley and the barn door.

How long had he been listening? Holly wondered. How much had he heard?

CHAPTER 8

THE ANTIQUES' DEALER

Drudge wheezed and pulled out his handkerchief. "Ma Spears sent me out here to see if there was any bits and pieces I might could sell for her in my store." He wiped the sweat that dripped profusely from his forehead. Then he pushed his horn-rim glasses up off the bridge of his bulbous nose with his index finger. His bulging eyes quickly surveyed the inside of the barn. They did not miss the wooden barrel.

"Watcha got there?" he asked, stepping up to the kids.

"Nothing!" Ethan answered, tightening the front line.

"You foster kids are all alike." His lip curled up over the top of his right eyetooth as he leaned his bushy eyebrows into their faces. He stared them down for a moment, then turned away from them and headed for the door. "Misfits, that's what you are. Onliest things you care about is yourselves." He looked back at them with contempt. "Don't give a care for nobody else. Man can't even make a decent living." Holly could hear Drudge mumbling as he left the barn and headed toward the road back to town.

"Whew! That was close." Drew exhaled.

Ethan high-fived Drew. "Great save, Drewster, getting Sací back into the barrel!"

"Why does Mr. Drudge want that smelly old barrel?" Ashley asked.

Holly picked it up and carefully began to examine it. "Well, the metal rings around it are probably brass. The cork looks like it was carved by hand." She turned it upside down forgetting that Sací was bumping around inside. Carved on the bottom were the words "Salvador, Bahia, 1810."

Ethan whistled.

There wasn't a sound in the barn.

Holly placed the barrel back in a dark corner of the barn. "We better cover this up with straw, so no one sees it."

After making sure the barrel was completely hidden, the four kids walked quietly out of the barn, each one heading in a separate direction to begin the day's chores.

CHAPTER 9

POOR LITTLE ELF

Holly had an eagle's view of the barn from her bedroom window where a fire escape hung down to the ground. Off in the distance, she could see the dock leading through the tidelands to the bay. Her room was outfitted with Maplewood furniture. There was a bunk bed in case there were more children needing to stay with Mom and Pop. For now, she was relieved to have the room to herself, so she slept on the bottom bunk. The room was also furnished with a chest of drawers, bedside table, desk, stuffed platform rocker, and her mother's cedar chest where she kept all her diaries. The old-fashioned wallpaper had a black background covered with pinkish brown and white flowers growing amidst a profusion of olive-green leaves and vines. The ceiling and the woodwork were painted white. The windows were crisscrossed with shear white priscilla curtains. The floors throughout the house were hardwood. An oval braided rug in soft, pastel colors covered most of the floor in her room. She never had such a lovely room to call her own.

As she was making up her bed, she glanced out the window and noticed Ashley walking toward the barn. She was carrying something small in her hand. Holly wondered why she would be going to the barn when she was supposed to be cleaning her room. Moments later, she saw Ashley running from the barn as if bats were flying after her. Holly ran down the stairs, two at a time, shot through the back door, and collided with Ashley before she reached the back porch.

"It's gone, Holly! It's gone. I looked everywhere. It's not there." Ashley dropped down on the back steps as tears ran down her face. In her hands she was holding some old doll clothes. "I wanted to dress Sací in case he's cold." She held up a little white cotton shirt, a short red jacket to match his cap, and small red woolen pants where she had cut off one leg. "The barrel is gone," Ashley repeated. Holly took her hand and they hurried back to the barn. Ashley was right. The barrel was nowhere in sight. Together they went in search of Drew and Ethan. They found them in the corral exercising Thumper and Juniper.

"Should we tell Mom Spears?" Holly asked after telling them that the barrel was missing.

"No!" Drew said.

"She'll fuss at us for keeping it a secret in the first place," Ethan said. *He brings hidden things to light!* He quoted in his best Mom Spears imitation.

Holly walked over to where they had covered the barrel. The straw was piled up but the barrel was gone. "I wonder if Drudge was lurking outside the barn just waiting for us to leave so he could poke around and see what we were trying to hide."

"Poor Saci," wailed Ashley. "He was my best friend."

"He was your only friend." Ethan chuckled.

Walking back and forth, Holly let out a deep sigh. "What'll we do now?"

All four heads turned toward the house as the bell clanged on the back porch. Mom Spears was calling them for lunch.

Ethan looked at Holly. "Nothing much we can do now, Carrot Cake. We'll just have to wait and see what happens. We're going to need time to think this one through."

Holly wondered how much time they had before someone would discover that the real treasure wasn't exactly the barrel, but what was *in* the barrel. And once having discovered him, what they would do with him. All of a sudden she remembered that she still had Saci's red cap and that meant that whoever found Saci was going to be in for a lot of trouble!

CHAPTER 10

HENRY DRUDGE'S DECEPTION

That evening at dinnertime, Holly placed an enormous casserole of macaroni and cheese on the table to accompany the pot of homegrown string beans and onions that Mom Spears had cooked with bacon.

"Sure is a treat to have Pop Spears join us for dinner this evenin'," Mom Spears said as she came up to the table, sliding her apron over her head. She patted her hair in a girlish way, blushing as she took her seat at the opposite end of the table from him. Holly noticed that she always acted that way when he was nearby. She didn't know why. He hardly looked like the type that would make a woman get all fl ushed and go red in the face. He had black hair that he wore slicked straight back, sharp black eyes, a face that pointed downward, a mustache that aimed upward, and a nose that projected outward, shaped like a hawk's beak. "Wash them hands, Ashley?" he asked in a tight, narrow voice as he presided over the dinner table.

Ashley studied her fingertips, not answering.

"Go wash them hands, Ash!" Mom Spears commanded, gently. "You know why."

"We all know why." Ethan rolled his eyes and pretended to pick his nose.

"I meant because cleanliness is next to godliness." Mom Spears frowned at Ethan over the rim of her bifocals.

Ashley made a record-breaking dash to the washroom and was back at the table in an instant, holding a wet hand out to Holly for grace. Pop Spears said the blessing. He made up for all the meals he missed while the food sat growing colder minute by minute. He ended with "God bless the work of our hands. Amen!"

"Amen!" They all chorused.

"And bless the homeless, the unjustly imprisoned, and . . ." Ethan added.

"And all black brothers and sisters!" Holly, Ashley, Drew, and Mom Spears shouted in unison.

Ethan hung his head, hiding his face under his dreadlocks. *He looked strangely beautiful,* Holly thought.

"Hear about what's happened to Drudge?" Pop Spears asked.

All the kids sat straight, ears tuned to the conversation.

"Mister Henry was around just yesterday, lookin' for odds and ends to sell on commission. I know his antique store ain't been doin' well," Mom Spears answered, handing the macaroni and cheese over to Drew.

"Well, it's gonna do mighty fine, now. They say he found this old rum barrel. Worth a fortune. Must have come over on a slave ship. The name Bellona is scratched on the brass ring around it," Pop Spears said.

"There was a Portuguese ship by that name that took a cargo of African slaves from Brazil to Mobile, or Pensacola, Florida in 1810 after the official abolition of the American slave trade in 1808." Excitement elevated Ethan's voice.

"How come you know so much?" Drew asked, holding his fork in midair. Everyone at the table looked at Ethan.

"There's a slave ship database on the Internet," Ethan mumbled, again lowering his head while pushing string beans onto his plate.

"And just how did you get on the Internet, son?" Pop Spears frowned, his eyes squeezed into a tight squint.

"I used your computer after you went to bed, sir" Ethan confessed, setting down his fork and looking straight into Pop Spears' eyes. Pop Spears stared at Ethan for a long moment. No one breathed. All hands stopped passing dishes around the table.

"Next time ask permission, you hear? A man doesn't take without askin'. Not for hungry stomachs and not for hungry minds. You don't take and then bear the consequences. You ask and then deal with the outcome." Pop Spears gave Ethan a slight, rare smile.

There was a collective sigh. Hands began passing the food

again. Cutlery clattered against dishes. Dinnertime chatter picked up its momentum.

"Where'd Drudge find the barrel?" asked Mom Spears, after taking a long thirsty swallow of her homemade lemonade. Normally she wiped her mouth with the back of her hand. In Pop Spears' presence, however, she daintily dabbed at the corners of her mouth with her thumb and forefinger.

"Says he found it hereabouts." Pop Spears stuffed a spoonful of macaroni into his mouth. "About the same time, though, some weird things started happenin'. Rumor has it a couple of his valuable first editions got all tore up. One of his prized porcelain vases cracked." He wiped his thin lips with his wide napkin. "A fellow over to the chicken plant said that some guy from the bank visited Drudge yesterday afternoon to collect his late mortgage payment, which, by the way, Drudge didn't have. When the guy went to leave, he tripped over his own feet and fell down the stairs. His shoelaces was tied together."

Holly glanced sideways at Drew, who was eyeing Ethan, who was eyeballing the ceiling. Ashley opened her mouth as though to call out something, and Holly quickly packed a slice of bread into it, giving her a look of warning.

After dinner chores were finished, the kids headed out to the barn for a meeting.

"We've got to get Sací and the barrel back!" Holly shoved her hands onto her hips and pressed her face into the triangle made by Ethan, Drew, and Ashley.

"And just how do you propose we do that?" Drew asked.

"Let's meet up in my room after Mom and Pop Spears go to sleep." Holly suggested. "We can sneak out and go into town to Drudge's store. We'll get Sací and the barrel and hide it back in the barn. Old man Drudge will never know what happened to it."

"The floorboards squeak. They'll hear us walking through the kitchen," Ethan reminded them.

"Not if you crawl under the kitchen table," Ashley said. Three pairs of eyes stared at her.

"Oops," she said, looking away and scuffing her foot in the dirt.

Drew threw up his hands. "Even if we make it to the door, the screen door creaks. We'll never get out without waking them."

"We will if we use the fire escape in my room," Holly said, with a sly smile. She watched the possibility of success spread onto everyone's face, and they put their heads together as they planned the rescue mission.

CHAPTER 11

DOWN THE FIRE ESCAPE

Hours later, gathered in Holly's room, the four prepared to descend the fi re escape.

"I'll go fi rst," Drew said. "Holly, you come down after me. Then Ashley, so Ethan can help her out the window."

"Who's going to help me?" Ethan asked. "I don't like heights. Not that I'm afraid or anything like that. It's just the whole concept of gravity that's unappealing."

"You either have to go fi rst or you have to go last. Pick one!" Drew muttered through clenched teeth.

"Okay. Last. That way, if I fall, you all can catch me." A huge grin spread across Ethan's face.

"Yea, a fire drill," Ashley whispered, starting for the window, headfirst. Holly grabbed the waistband of her pants and pulled her back into the room.

Slowly, beneath the beam of a full, late August moon, Holly watched Drew's descent down the fire escape. Boswell waited at the bottom, with his snoot lifted upward, howling at this intrusion into his domain.

"Quiet!" whispered Drew, nearing the ground. "Good boy!" He congratulated the hound, scratching its long, floppy ears.

Next, Holly slipped through the window. Stepping gingerly onto the fire escape, she held her breath as she missed the first rung. After a scary balancing act, she steadied herself. Ethan helped Ashley get up to the windowsill while Holly pulled her through. When they reached the ground, Holly looked up and realized that Ethan was stuck halfway through the window.

"I can't get through," he whispered down to the others.

"Yes, you can. Hurry up!" Drew hissed.

"Can't. Go on without me," Ethan said softly, with an air of defeat.

"Oh! For crying out loud. . ." Drew said under his breath as he headed back up the fire escape to collect Ethan.

A light blinked on in Mom and Pop's second-floor bedroom. Drew froze on the fire escape, just below Ethan. Holly grabbed Ashley and they flattened themselves to the side of the house, under the open window.

"Did ya hear that sound, Mother?"

The answer emerged from the depths of the room. "That I did. That I did."

"Sounds like it come from thisaway," Father Spears said,

his voice getting louder.

Holly could picture him pulling the curtains apart and looking out onto the yard. She hugged Ashley tightly to the house and held her breath.

"Ownliest thing I see yonder is that dumb dog," she heard him say.

"Come back to bed, dear. It's nothin' to be afeard of. Kids are safe. Probably just the critter." After what seemed like an eternity, Holly peaked up at the window. The light was out. She looked up the ladder at Drew and gave him a *thumbs up*. He helped Ethan pull his other leg through the window, then the rest of his body followed. Quietly, they began their descent to the ground.

After a one-hour hike, the four arrived at the steps of Drudge's Antiques. The street was deserted. The shop sat back off the street, surrounded by laurel bushes, gone wild. In front of the shop window grew a crepe myrtle the size of a tree, covered with blossoms that looked ash gray in the moonlight. A weeping willow dragged ghostly shapes across the yard as the late-night winds quickened. Heavy clouds stretched over the face of the moon like taut rubber bands, holding the circle of light together. A sticker pasted to the front door read "This building is protected by Security Alarms."

"Now what?" Drew shadowed his face from the fading moonlight as he peered into the shop window.

"Saci." Ashley whispered loudly, pushing herself in front of Drew and peeking through the bottom of the window. "Where are you?"

Out of the darkness, he appeared. He grinned up at them from the other side of the window, springing up and down on his leg and clapping his hands together. *He is a picture of total joy,* Holly thought, breathing a sigh of relief at the sight of him.

"We came to get you out and bring you back home with us," Holly explained through the window. She glanced nervously over her shoulder as a car sped by.

"How are we going to get in?" Drew asked, in a low whisper. "The alarm is probably set. If it goes off, we won't be able to get Sací and the barrel out of there before the police catch us."

"With my luck, I'll end up in juvie, kissing my future career as a history teacher good-bye," moaned Ethan.

Holly heard the crunch of stones under tires as a police car slowly approached the shop. At once, the four of them dove toward the darkest side of the building and crouched low to the ground. The car rolled to a stop. It sat there for a while with the motor idling. Holly's heart pounded in her chest until she thought it would blow up. Finally, the car pulled away and headed down the street, the engine rumbling off into the distance.

Slowly, the four moved from their hiding places and returned to the shop window.

Holly peered through the window. Her eyes searched over the walls of the room, locating the alarm box on the wall near the door. She could see the red light shining brightly, notifying her that the alarm was indeed set to go off if an intruder opened a window or a door.

"Sací, did you by any chance see Drudge put in the alarm code?" she asked.

"Code? What does it mean, code?" he answered.

Holly's shoulders sagged.

"When Drudge left, he went to the box on the wall and pushed some buttons. Did you see which buttons he pushed?" Drew asked through the window.

"Yes, yes. I see the buttons he push," Sací answered, smiling and nodding.

Holly's hope surged. "Do you remember what they were?"

"Yes, yes. I remember." Sací again nodded his head.

Holly and Drew looked at each other. "Well, could you push them?" They both asked impatiently.

Sací jumped across the room and leaped up to the alarm box. Using the mouthpiece of his pipe, he quickly jabbed at the buttons. The red light went to green. Holly tried the doorknob, hoping that it might not be locked but it was bolted.

"Do you know if he keeps a spare key around?" Ethan asked through the window.

Sací hopped over to Drudge's desk in the back of the room, disappeared for a few seconds, and returned dragging a key slowly across the floor. He dropped it when he reached the door and looked up at them with both his palms raised upward in a questioning gesture.

"Push the key under the door!" Holly pointed down.

Drew snatched up the key as it slid under the door. He quickly unlocked the deadbolt and opened the door while Ethan stood watch. Ashley picked up Sací and placed him on her shoulder for the return trip.

"Where's the barrel, Sací?" Holly asked, frantically looking around.

"It is in back room where the mister Drudge cleans and polishes it." Sací pointed his pipe toward the back of the store.

Holly darted behind the heavy velvet curtain that separated the store from the workshop, yanked the barrel and the cork off the workbench, and ran for the street. Ashley and Ethan followed her. They watched while Drew closed and locked the door. He wiped off the key with his shirttail and slipped it back under the door. Holly removed Sací from Ashley and wedged him into the barrel. After replacing the cork they headed for home, grateful for the thick misty clouds that now covered the moon.

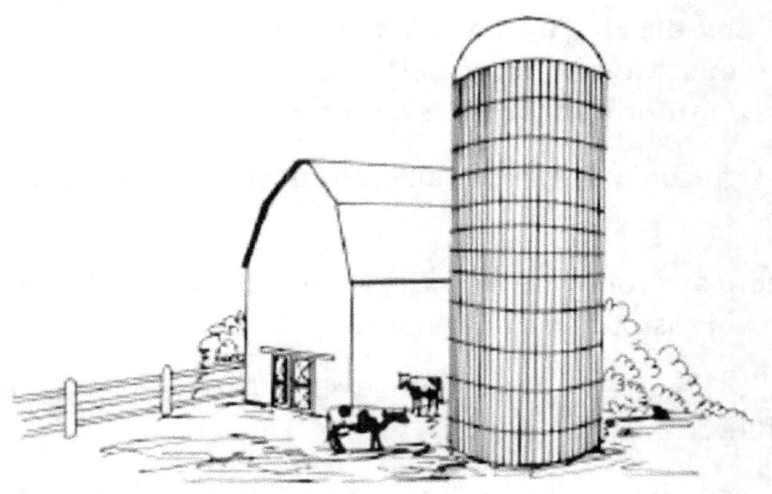

CHAPTER 12

HATCHING A PLAN

"Mother, we must make sure the doors are locked tonight. You kids make sure your windows are closed and locked. I heard strange noises last night, and they were sayin' at the plant today that poor Drudge has been robbed," Pop Spears said as they sat around the dinner table.

"Why, who ever heard of such goins' on here in these parts." Mom Spears clicked her tongue and shook her head.

"The men are sayin' that some man from New York City showed up with a check for twenty thousand dollars to buy that rum barrel from Drudge for a museum. Drudge was countin' on that money to save his business. Now that the barrel's gone missing, only the good Lord knows what's goin' to save him from bankruptcy." Pop Spears' eyes turned heavenward, and his lips curved downward giving his face a sorrowful appearance.

"Oh, my dear! Pay no mind. God works in strange and mysterious ways. Praise be!" Mom Spears rejoiced as she shouted out orders for the evening's chores.

"Be right back," Ashley hollered as she headed toward the porch.

"Where are you goin' with those beans, child?" Mom Spears' eyebrows rose to meet her hairline.

"I'm. . .I'm. . .They're for Boswell." The words rushed out of Ashley.

"Boswell don't like beans." Mom Spears' face registered clear rejection of the idea.

"He loves them." Ashley shouted as she ran out the door.

"Kid is goin' to kill that critter!" Mom Spears shook her head.

"I'll make sure she doesn't give him too much," Holly said as she rushed out to join Ashley.

Holly could hear Ethan and Drew chime in. "I better make sure she doesn't give any to Thumper and Juniper."

"Me, too."

Both boys slammed through the back door, following Holly and Ashley to the barn.

They turned on the light in the barn and checked to make sure the barrel was still safely out of sight.

"Now what are we going to do?" Holly asked the others as they all sat down. "Even though Drudge stole the barrel from us, we can't just let him lose his business."

"And we should care? He's never done anything for us.

He doesn't even like us!" Drew spit out the words. "Why should Drudge be entitled to all that money? Look how hard Mom and Pop Spears work. They do so much for us and get little money for doing it." Drew stuffed his hands into his pockets. "When my parents were alive, I had everything." He hesitated. "When they died, I had nothing. There was no one. When Social Services placed me here, I wished I'd died with my parents. I thought these people were so weird."

"Well, they are, sort of," Ethan said, grinning. "But they're good people, too."

"I've come to see that," said Drew. "I see how hard they work to look after us. They're kind even when they discipline us. I may no longer have everything, but I have all that I need."

"They're sure the best foster family I've lived with." Holly added. "Maybe we should talk to Drudge. Tell him that we know he stole the barrel from the Pop's barn." Holly glanced around the circle to see everyone's reaction.

Ethan slapped his fist into his hand. "We could strike a deal with him. He could have the barrel back if he agrees to share the money from the sale with Mom and Pop Spears."

"I don't want Sací to lose his little house." Ashley cried.

"We'll get him another house. He doesn't have to live in a rum barrel for the rest of his life." Ethan said.

Ashley's eyes lit up. "We could put him in a birdhouse; one that's big enough for him to have his very own bed, and table, and chairs."

"Let's not get carried away." Ethan rolled his eyes.

Ashley pulled the cork out of the barrel and hollered into the opening. "What do you think, Sací?"

"I think that I will like to eat more beans." Sací stifled a small burp just before Ashley sealed the barrel back up. "See, I knew he wanted those beans."

The next morning, Holly, Ashley, and Sací waited in the barn for Drew and Ethan to arrive. Holly brushed Thumper and Juniper while Ashley darted around the barn, moving from one chore to another without completing any of them, all the while sustaining a heart-to-heart with Sací.

Holly paused her brushing. "Ashley, can't you just be quiet for a little while?"

"I'm sorry. I don't mean to make noise." Ashley froze in place for a fraction of a second with round eyes raised toward Holly.

Sací was riding Boswell around and around the barn, bouncing up and down like a bronco rider in a rodeo competition. He clung to the dog's collar with all his might, straddling him with his one leg. With a sudden burst of energy, Ashley began chasing after them. The three collided into Ethan and Drew as they pushed through the barn door.

"Tone it down!" Ethan ordered. "Do you want us to get caught?"

Drew plunged the wooden cork into the rum barrel, wrapped the barrel with newspaper, and nestled it carefully into the basket on his bike.

"*Ooé*, where you take my house?" Sací cried.

"Don't worry about it. We'll get you a better house. You'll like it. Promise." Ethan answered lifting the kickstand on his bike and following Drew out the door.

Holly and Ashley trailed behind on their bikes, pedaling as fast as they could to keep up.

"Wait for me!" Sací shouted. His one leg moved him faster than Holly's bike was traveling. With a swift leap, he catapulted into the air and landed on the backpack that she had tossed into the basket of her bike before leaving. "You'll have to hide, Sací. We don't want anyone to see you," she said as they sped on their way.

"*Certo.* Okay. I go to hide," Sací said, crawling into one of the pockets of the backpack.

The wind blew through Holly's hair. The morning was so quiet she could hear the birds chirp. Small black and red chickens pecked at food along the roadside. They came to the rickety bridge that crossed a creek approaching Drudge's property when all of a sudden, they heard "Noooooooo!" All four kids slammed on their breaks.

Sací's body was trembling, his eyes were huge, darting to and from the creek. "You no can to take me over water. I tell you my fear. I stay this side and hide and wait for you."

"But Sací, you've crossed this bridge before," Holly said.

"You were even in the ocean." Ethan added.

"But I was safe in barrel with cross on cork. What keep me safe now?" Sací looked frantic, waving his pipe around.

"We can't put him in the barrel now because we're giving the barrel to Drudge. We sure don't want to give him Sací." Drew tightened his hold on the barrel in his bicycle carrier.

"I know!" Ashley pulled a little medal out of her pocket. "Here, Sací. This medal has a tiny bird on it. A little dove. The dove visited the Son of God when he came up out of the water of his baptism and it kept him safe. It will keep Son of Wind safe, too."

Saci grabbed the medal and disappeared into the pocket

of Holly's backpack. "Okay. Let's go. This plan has got to work," Holly said.

But what if the plan didn't work, Holly mused as she pedaled along the road. The only answer was the sound coming back of bicycle pedals driving bicycle tires around and around, crunching down gravel as they moved toward their destination.

CHAPTER 13

STRIKING A DEAL

Drudge's Antiques looked different in the morning. Sunlight had wiped away the spooky shadows and the mist. The fl owers on the crepe myrtle had changed from gray to pink. A sign hung in the door that read "Inventory Sale—50% Off All Items."

The kids parked their bikes. Drew lifted their precious cargo out of his carrying basket. Holly put on her backpack, careful not to crush Sací.

The kids opened the door and walked in. There were no customers in the store.

"Mr. Drudge!" Holly called out. "Mr. Drudge, are you here?" Finally he appeared through the heavy velvet curtain. The dark circles under his eyes matched his horn-rimmed glasses.

"What do you want?" Drudge asked, throwing his head up and jutting out his whiskered chin.

"We heard you lost something," Drew said. He leaned against the counter and looked Drudge directly in the eyes.

"But then you can't lose something that was never yours in the first place, can you?" Ethan asked, squaring his bulk up in front of Drudge. "They put people in prison for stealing things, you know. Sometimes innocent people end up paying for it." There was a catch in Ethan's voice and angry tears in his eyes. He held his arms straight down by his sides, but his hands were clenched in a fist that he kept opening and closing.

Holly realized that Ethan must be thinking of his father. She had no idea that he would react this way. Quickly, she stepped up to Drudge, forcing Ethan to step back. "We're here to make a deal with you," she said. "We know you took that rum barrel out of Pop's barn. We know because I'm the one that found it on the beach and hid it in the barn."

"Ma Spears said I could have anything I found out there," Drudge said, defensively.

"On commission," Ethan said. "But you were going to take that whole twenty thousand dollars from the museum people and save your own hide. I'll bet you were never even going to tell Mom and Pop Spears that it came out of their barn. Right?" Ethan crossed his arms.

Drudge ran his crooked fingers over his greasy head. Pulling out his handkerchief, he began to mop his face and neck.

"Here's the deal." Drew handed over his package. "Mom and Pop Spears get half."

Drudge slowly removed the newspaper. Holding the barrel as if it were a newborn baby, he began to sputter. Drool oozed from the corners of his mouth. His breathing became rapid. His mouth hung open as he stared fixedly at the object in his hands. He collapsed into a nearby chair and lifted his scraggly head to look hard at the kids. There was full-blown relief in his bloodshot eyes. "Oh my, you sure threw a wrinkle at me! I guess I was plenty wrong about you foster kids! I don't hardly know what to say. My store was going bust. I would have been penniless and I thought I'd found a treasure that would save me. I was so relieved I got greedy. Then of a sudden when the barrel disappeared the dream crashed, and I knew I was goin' under. I don't know how I can ever thank you." Drudge hung his head as he cradled the barrel.

"Remember! Half. Fifty percent. If Mom and Pop Spears don't hear this promise from you before the day is over, there's a little black gremlin that's going to make you wish you had." Ethan threatened, glancing at Holly's backpack.

"Heh?" Mr. Drudge looked up from the barrel.

"Never mind," Holly said.

Ashley pointed to a large white birdhouse sitting on a shelf in the corner of the store. "Mr. Drudge, may we have that?"

Drudge walked over to the birdhouse, lifted it off the shelf, examined it, and handed it over to Ashley. "Well, it ain't really no antique anyway. It's just an old birdhouse. Sure, I reckon you can have it."

"Thank you!" Ashley said, grabbing it from his hand and smiling up at him.

"Thank *you!*" he said, quietly. "All of you!"

As the kids were leaving the store, they heard a clatter and a wail of protest coming from Mr. Drudge who was laying at the foot of the front steps with his shoelaces tied together. Ashley ran back to help him up. She brushed the dirt from his clothes and helped him remove the knot from his laces. Holly caught site of Sací climbing into the birdhouse, now positioned in the basket on Ashley's bike. She scolded him with her eyes. He answered with a grin as he slipped out of sight.

CHAPTER 14

THE MAGIC OF RED

"What are we ever goin' to do with ten thousand dollars? Imagine pastor's face when we put one tenth of that in the collection plate this Sunday! One thousand dollars might could help put the new roof on the church," Pop Spears exclaimed.

"The Lord be praised! *He performs wonders that can't be understood, miracles that can't be counted.'* Mom Spears clasped her hands to her ample bosom.

The kids left Mom and Pop Spears sitting alone at the supper table, holding hands. As they headed toward the barn, Holly could hear their voices coming through the screen door, talking about what they were going to do with all that money.

By now, meeting in the barn was becoming a tradition. Holly smiled as she realized how quickly she had begun to look forward to it, like candied apples on Halloween and turkey on Thanksgiving. "My heart feels so full," she said, taking a deep satisfying breath. She pulled the moment into herself in a great gulp of air so she could capture it for all the years to come. She determined to put the whole experience into words in her diary so she would never forget.

"Ah, my head feel so cold," Sací remarked with a shrug, looking at Holly with the palms of his hands raised upward. His empty pipe bobbed up and down as he sucked on it, vigorously.

They all laughed.

"I guess it's time to give you your powers back. We can't hold on to your red cap forever," Holly said to Sací wistfully.

"Wish I had a red cap," Ethan muttered. "Or at least a Nike one," he said, eyeing Drew.

"Your hair wouldn't fit into it." Drew smacked Ethan on the back affectionately.

"You do have a red cap," Holly said. "We all do. We have a good home, a safe place, with people that care about us. We have each other. And we have a Heavenly Father. That's the best kind of power there is." There was a lump in her throat as she looked intensely around at the group. The three kids looked back at her, their expressions reflecting her words.

"I know! Let's make a pact!" Ashley jumped up. "We'll be the Sací kids forever and ever," she declared. "I promise to love you forever, Sací." She planted a sloppy kiss on the top of Sací's head, which he instantly rubbed off.

"I'll try to be more of a team player," Drew vowed. He dropped one of his homemade golf balls onto the barn floor and stood up, positioning his Tiger Woods Nike cap squarely on his head. He gripped his favorite golf club, placing it next to the ball. Jiggling his backside into just the right angle, he took a couple of practice swings. With dead-eye accuracy, he whooshed the ball smack into the hayloft. Holly and Ashley cheered. Ethan let out a whistle. Boswell lifted his snoot up and barked.

"When I become a teacher, I'm going to include Brazil in my lessons about slavery," Ethan said. He stood straight with his huge right hand flat against his broad chest and his face raised to the ceiling, as though he were pledging allegiance to the flag. "I hereby declare myself multicultural history teacher extraordinaire."

Drew joined him, holding an imaginary microphone. "May I present to you my gifted friend and colleague, the inimitable Doctor Ethan Owens, renowned Professor of African History."

The Sací kids applauded.

"I promise to write about you, Sací, until I'm an old lady and can't see or hold a pencil anymore." Holly pretended to write with her diary held up close to her eyes. "When I'm a famous, published author, Americans everywhere will know about you." Looking at Sací, she asked him "What do you promise? Will you stay with us if we give you your magical cap back?" Hesitating, she dug into her pocket for the red cap and reluctantly placed it on his tiny head.

Sací raised his shoulders and let them fall as though he were filled with joy. Removing his pipe from his mouth, he smiled his toothy grin. His eyes twinkled. *"Quem sabe?* Who knows? Life is chancy. Who can say where it lead you? One day I seasick on slave ship, next day I bobbing along on bicycle. Tomorrow?"

Leaves and straw began to rise in a cloud of dust that moved around and around the barn. The ground began to shake, and the barn began to tremble. Immediately, spinning into a whirlwind, Sací disappeared into thin air.

Ethan looked at Drew. "Well, Drewster, at least this time there's no rotten egg smell."

"That's because now he's not afraid of us," Ashley said. Tears ran down her face.

"Maybe he'll let us be his foster family," Holly said. "We'll leave the birdhouse in the tree in case he comes back some day."

They all agreed.

Ashley reminded them that one of Sací's disguises was a songbird. "Who knows, he might be in his new home right now."

Walking toward the house, Holly turned to look at the birdhouse silhouetted against the sunset. It was fastened to the branch of an old pine tree that stood on the shore overlooking the dock. It would be a new home for Sací, if he stayed, or when he visited. Just like Mom and Pop Spears had made a new home for her and the others—a shelter that no longer seemed like a prison but rather like a happy home with a family. She touched her medal of Our Lady Who Appeared. Miracles. Yes, perhaps she should believe in miracles . . . afterall, it was sort of awesome she was placed in this pretty house, with such a kind family, with great friends, and Sací . . . the greatest miracle of all.

Far off in the distance, coming from the direction of the tidelands, the Sací kids heard "Cee-e-e," like the sighing of the wind or the singing of a bird.

But they knew it wasn't the wind.

And they knew it wasn't a bird.

They knew it was Saci, whistling his call to arms.

Travelers and strangers beware – you never know when Saci will visit you. If weird and wonderful things begin to happen around you, be sure to blame it on Saci.

"Saci made me do it." "I didn't do it, Saci did it." Because he almost certainly did!

EPILOGUE

(In memory of my brother, Raphael Caccese, Jr. 1959-2017)

The ending of my story reminds me of a popular Brazilian folksong that I used to sing to my younger brother who we called Raphaelzinho, *Little Ralph*. The folksong is about a little girl and a shy songbird called a *Sabiá* (Thrush) that lives in a birdcage in her backyard. One day Sabiá makes a tiny hole to escape his cage and flies away to sing in an avocado tree. The little girl who loves him feels sad and cries for Sabiá to come back to her. She tells him she's waiting for him and he tells her to stop crying because he is coming back. I wonder, could the Sabiá of this folksong be the Sací of this story in disguise?

The tune "Sabiá lá na Gaiola," was composed by Mário Vieira (1921-1999) and Hervé Cordovil (1914-1979). This Brazilian *sertanejo* "backcountry" genre is the equivalent of America's country music and is possibly even more popular in style than the Brazilian Samba. The predominant sound in the music is the viola.

For further information on the song go to <u>https:// pt.wikipedia.org/wiki/Sabiá_na_Gaiola</u>.

For the lyrics and music go to <u>Sabiá Lá Na Gaiola - Grupo</u>

BIBLIOGRAPHY

Cascudo, Luis da Camara. *Dicionário do Folclore Brasileiro.* Belo Horizone, Brasil: Editora Itatiaia, Ltda., 1993.

Giácomo, Maria Thereza Cunha de. *O Saci-Pererê.* São Paulo, Brasil: Edições Melhoramentos, 1974.

Larousse Cultural. *Brasil A/Z: Enciclopédia Alfabética em um Único Volume.* São Paulo, Brasil: Editora Universo, 1998.

Lobato, Monteiro. *O Saci.* São Paulo, Brasil: Editora Brasiliense, S.A., 1975.

[Lobato, Monteiro]. *O Sacy Perêrê: Resultado de um Inquerito.* [Brasil?]: s.n., [1917].

Nalon, Jose Alexandre and "the Psychedelic Goblin" (Colin Chapman). *Saci.*   www.trf.se/old_trfsite/rpg/changeling/ kiths/saci.htm.

Queiroz, Renato da Silva. *Um Mito Bem Brasileiro: Estudo Antropológico Sobre o Saci.* São Paulo, Brasil: Livraria e Editora Polis Ltds., 1987.

"Saci (Brazilian Folklore)." *Wikepedia,* the Free Encyclopedia. Saci (Brazilian folklore) - Wikipedia

Santos, Eurico. *História, Lendas, e Folklore de Nossos Bichos.* Belo Horizonte, Brasil: Editora Itatiaia, Ltda., 1987.

www.ingramcontent.com/pod-product-compliance
Lightning Source LLC
Chambersburg PA
CBHW071951190726
48293CB00004B/1423